For Eli and Hannah – GPR

Created exclusively for World International Limited by Bloomsbury Publishing Plc
First published in Great Britain in 1997 by World International Limited, Deanway
Technology Centre, Wilmslow Road, Handforth, Cheshire SK9 3FB

Copyright © Text Mary Hooper 1997
Copyright © Illustrations Guy Parker-Rees 1997
Art Direction Lisa Coombes

The moral right of the author and illustrator has been asserted
A CIP catalogue record of this book is available from the
British Library

ISBN 0 7498 3090 5

Printed by Bath Press, Great Britain

10 9 8 7 6 5 4 3 2 1

Little Readers

SLOW DOWN SALLY

Mary Hooper

Pictures by Guy Parker-Rees

World International Limited

Sally always did everything in a rush and a hurry.
But on Saturday morning she was really terrible.

She got up at six o'clock and woke
Mummy and Daddy . . .

"Oh, Sally! Whatever time do you call this?"

Then she sprinted into the bathroom. She tickled her two front teeth with her brush – beating her *fastest-ever* record for teeth-cleaning . . .

. . . and washed her face so *quickly* that
the flannel didn't even get wet.

She got dressed in such a hurry she put her clothes on back to front.

And she shot down
   the banisters so *speedily*
   that she scorched her bottom.

She *hared* down the hall,
tore into the kitchen like
a tornado and frightened
Archie the cat out of
the window.

Then she ran across the kitchen, tripped over Rufus the dog's bowl and sent it skimming along the floor.

She *raced* to the cupboard,

emptied the cereal
into her mouth

and then swallowed
some milk.

She made herself some toast –

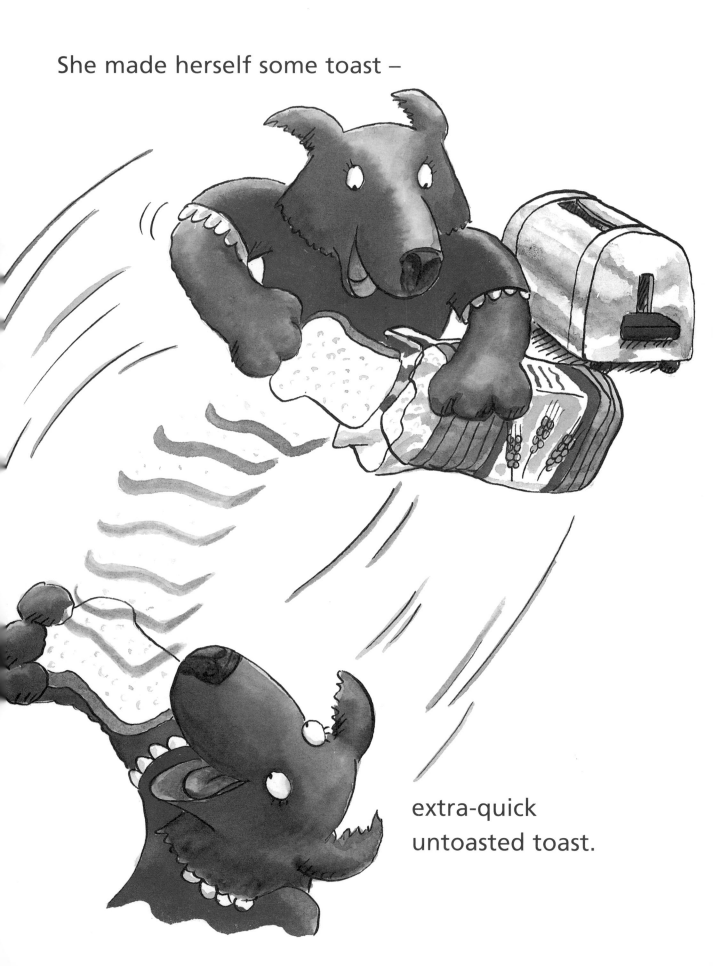

extra-quick
untoasted toast.

Running to the door to let Rufus out, she skidded on some dog food, grabbed the tablecloth and sent everything flying.

And then she took Rufus
for such a fast walk round
the garden that his paws
never touched the ground.

She ran into the sitting room to do her
special job, which was cleaning out the bird cage.

She *whisked* the lining paper from
under Billy's feet so swiftly he did
two somersaults in the air and
landed head first in his water bowl.

Then Sally thought she'd go out on her bike.

"I'm going out for a ride!"
she shouted up to
Mummy and Daddy.

"Sally! Just a minute!"
Mummy shouted, but
Sally was already *racing*
out of the front door.

She called for her friend Toni, but was
gone by the time anyone came to the door.

And then she *zoomed* up and down the pavement several times,

going at such speed
people thought they'd
been passed by a motor bike.

When she got home,
she thought it must be
about time for lunch,

so she *gobbled* a
slice of bread,

then a slice of ham,

then another slice
of bread.

Orange squash would go nicely with her sandwich, Sally thought.

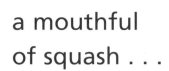

So she took a *gulp* of water,

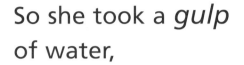

a mouthful of squash . . .

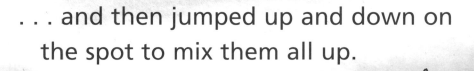

. . . and then jumped up and down on
the spot to mix them all up.

Mummy always liked her to do a spot of quiet reading after lunch, so Sally found her little brother's rag book.

Television was boring so Sally
did a quick picture. Then she
decided it must be time for bed.

She *galloped* up the stairs, getting undressed as she went . . .

Mummy came in.
"What IS all this?
What's going on?"
"Bedtime!" Sally panted.
"Hasn't the day gone quickly!"

"It has for you," Mummy said.
"What ARE you playing at?"

Sally snuggled down. "It's my
birthday tomorrow, so I'm in a
hurry to get today over and done with."

"Well," Mummy said. "YOU might have got today over and done with – but no one else has. It's only half-past seven in the morning!"

"Oh NO!" said Sally. "I've got to do everything all over again!"